... THE ADVENTURE STARTS HERE ...

TALES FROM GREAT BRITAIN

First published in Great Britain in 2009 by
Young Writers, Remus House, Coltsfoot Drive,
Peterborough, PE2 9JX
Tel (01733) 890066 Fax (01733) 313524
All Rights Reserved

Disclaimer
Young Writers has maintained every effort
to publish stories that will not cause offence.
Any stories, events or activities relating to individuals
should be read as fictional pieces and not construed
as real-life character portrayal.

FOREWORD

Since Young Writers was established in 1990, our aim has been to promote and encourage written creativity amongst children and young adults. By giving aspiring young authors the chance to be published, Young Writers effectively nurtures the creative talents of the next generation, allowing their confidence and writing ability to grow.

With our latest fun competition, *The Adventure Starts Here...* , primary school children nationwide were given the tricky challenge of writing a story with a beginning, middle and an end in just fifty words.

The diverse and imaginative range of entries made the selection process a difficult but enjoyable task with stories chosen on the basis of style, expression, flair and technical skill. A fascinating glimpse into the imaginations of the future, we hope you will agree that this entertaining collection is one that will amuse and inspire the whole family.

CONTENTS

THE MINI SAGAS

NO DINNER TONIGHT

Claire invited Greg for tea. He came because he was greedy. Where hens live it is dusty because hens like dustbaths. So Claire told Greg, 'Go and wash your paws,' and by the time he had got back, Claire had eaten all the food. He'd been tricked. He went home.

OLIVIA PARSONS (10)
Adderley CE Primary School, Market Drayton

1

THREE LITTLE PIGS

One pig made a house out of straw, another made a house out of sticks and the last was out of bricks. A wolf came. The first house came down and the second. They ran to the third house, Wolf followed. He couldn't blow it down so he gave up!

CHARLOTTE HAND (10)

Adderley CE Primary School, Market Drayton

2

THE KRAKEN

I said to my crew, 'Only ten boats have ever got
this far,' but I was worried because a beast lived
in the waters and it was owned by Davy Jones.
It was called The Kraken and it could kill a man.
Then ... *bang!* It got us!

JOLYON DIXON (9)

Adderley CE Primary School, Market Drayton

THE GINGERBREAD MAN

Long ago there was an old lady baking some gingerbread men. But when she removed them from the oven one jumped out and ran away. He met a pig. The pig was hungry and chased him. The gingerbread man said, 'Wee, wee, you can't catch me!' But he did.

TOM MORGAN (8)

Dorrington CE Primary School, Dorrington

LATE DUMPTY

Humpty Dumpty sat on a gate. Humpty Dumpty was very late. He had forgotten his cake, so he had to eat steak. But it was a long wait! So Humpty Dumpty went to a fete, but even there he was late! So Humpty Dumpty went home and sighed, 'Oh great!'

MAE GREEN (8)

Dorrington CE Primary School, Dorrington

5

HUMPTY DUMPTY

One freezing day Humpty Dumpty slipped off
a huge wall. He cracked so badly that when
one single person touched him he cracked into
hundreds of pieces. Everyone tried to put him
together but it was no use.
He died two weeks later in a small busy hospital.

ROSE BARNES (8)
Dorrington CE Primary School, Dorrington

A NIGHTMARE

I was in a London shopping centre. It was the 10th December. I had gone shopping for Christmas presents. Suddenly I went missing. I was panicking and panicking. I was scared. I was looking for my mum everywhere. I tried to ring my mum. Luckily it was a dream.

JAEDON LEWIS (10)
Dorrington CE Primary School, Dorrington

A LIFETIME DREAM

I sat desperately, impatiently waiting for the dreaded news. I clutched my ticket with hope in my heart, although there was always a little doubt trying to infect it. I watched carefully, clutching my ticket so hard it nearly ripped. I stood up proudly, I'd won, I'd won the lottery!

REBECCA DAISY BARNES (11)
Dorrington CE Primary School, Dorrington

NEW SCHOOL

It was my first day at school, I had no one to reassure me. My teacher seemed nice, but the children were teasing me. I wanted my mum. I was thinking of running away, but I didn't. I was a good girl. These big girls were coming towards me ... 'Hi!'

CATHERINE HUGHES (9)

Dorrington CE Primary School, Dorrington

9

A CHRISTMAS CAROL

Once upon a time lived a man called Ebenezer
Scrooge, he was a mean, cruel man and he hated
Christmas.
One night three ghosts came and they showed
him the past and the people who don't have
enough money to celebrate Christmas. So after
that day Mr Scrooge loved Christmas.

LYDIA ELLIS (9)
Dorrington CE Primary School, Dorrington

THE NIGHT OF HALLOWE'EN

It was the night of Hallowe'en. There was a creaky noise. All the doors flew open. Kayleigh went over to the light switch to turn the light on but it wouldn't go on. The doorbell rang and Kayleigh went to get the treats. 'Trick or treat?'

KAYLEIGH GOWARD (10)
Druridge Bay Middle School, South Broomhill

11

THE SPOOK

I climbed up my stairs and went to rest. Then five minutes later I heard a knock on my door. I opened it and a horrible face met my eyes. The face had big sharp teeth and wobbly eyes. I was scared. Then, 'Trick or treat?'

JACOB CROOKS (9)
Druridge Bay Middle School, South Broomhill

BEHIND THE DOOR

There is a *creak!* There is a *smash!* What's behind the door? Is it a bear? Is it a ghost? Is it a vampire or what is it? Could be just a tree. Let's find out and see. 'Argh!' There's a letter, could it be … ? *Open me!* it says.

KIRSTY ARMSTRONG (9)
Druridge Bay Middle School, South Broomhill

THE FOOTBALL MATCH

I kicked the ball and nearly scored. I was so close.
I should have guessed their keeper was really
good but then this huge person kicked the ball
straight at me. I did not know what to do. Then I
realised he was only passing me the ball!

NATHAN MOSSMAN (9)

Druridge Bay Middle School, South Broomhill

EMBARRASSMENT

I was chatting to my friend whilst getting ready for PE.
I was in my T-shirt and knickers. I was just about to
put my shorts on when the fire alarm went off. I put
my arms up and ran outdoors. *Oops* - in my knickers.
My crush was there!

GEMMA MURRAY (9)

Druridge Bay Middle School, South Broomhill

CHRISTMAS DAY

Suddenly Rachel woke up! She shouted, 'Yippee!'
Rachel went running into her parents' room,
giving them a fright. 'Can I open my presents
now?' screamed Rachel.
'No!' Mum said.
'Please! Please! Please!' Rachel begged.
'No! and that's the end of it, OK?' said Dad.
'Please!' Rachel shouted angrily.

ABBY SHELDON (10)

Druridge Bay Middle School, South Broomhill

HALLOWE'EN NIGHT

It was Hallowe'en and the boy called Mark came down the stairs in his costume. His mum laughed, his dad sneezed and the dog barked. Then he ran out the door and screamed. He ran next door. The man opened the door, got some sweets and screamed, 'Happy Hallowe'en!'

NATASHA JENNINGS (10)
Druridge Bay Middle School, South Broomhill

THE FRIGHT

'Mum, I'm home!' There was no answer. 'Mum,
where are you?' I was frightened. 'Mum, Dad?'
I was all alone on Hallowe'en. I shouted again,
'Mum, Dad, anyone? I'm scared.'
Someone knocked on the door. I answered.
Someone was there. *'Boo!'* shouted Mum. It was
Mum all along.

SHAE MERIFIELD (9)
Druridge Bay Middle School, South Broomhill

BOO!

There was a creak. 'Uh-oh,' I said. 'Charlie?' No
answer. I knew I shouldn't have left him. I walked
upstairs into his bedroom, opened the door and
there was no one there. I shut the door and
shouted again, 'Charlie?'
'Boo!'
'Argh!' I screamed.
He was behind me!

MEGGY FRATER (9)
Druridge Bay Middle School, South Broomhill

19

THE NOISE

Katy was walking down the bumpy road again to get home. Then she heard something in the bush. Katy said to herself, *probably an animal*, and she kept on walking. When she got to the house she heard the noises again, closer. Then out jumped her school friend, Lily.

FRANCESCA WATSON (9)

Druridge Bay Middle School, South Broomhill

FIREWORKS

Bang! Bang! That's all you could hear. Every second. *Bang! Bang!* All animals terrified and shaking inside the warm houses. And from the bottom of the stairs my dad shouts, 'Jasmin quick, the rabbit is terrified of the noises from the fireworks.'
'I'm coming!' I shout.

JASMIN BENNETT (9)

Druridge Bay Middle School, South Broomhill

THE EVIL ICE CREAM MAN!

Two children on a hot day were playing in their garden. They heard an ice cream man. They rushed there. They wanted two ninety-nines, they said to the man. He gave them their ice creams. They had worms in! So they threw them at the freaky, horrible man!

BAILEY WEEDON (10)

Gillingham Primary School, Gillingham

THE SUNKEN TITANIC

One stormy night Josh and Seb jumped in the black electrifying sea with scuba-diving gear on, to discover the sunken Titanic. As they explored, they went in and a tiger shark shot out and bit Josh's finger off. It snapped Seb's foot and both were never seen again.

JOSH ELLIS

Gillingham Primary School, Gillingham

JORDAN AND THE RING

The hotel exploded with a loud *bang!* Jordan was chasing the bomber when he fell through the trapdoor. He was looking for a ring. Jordan tiptoed past the sleeping guards in the cellar. Spotting the priceless ring on a glass shelf he grabbed it. Running up the stairs, he escaped.

JORDAN PORCH (10)
Gillingham Primary School, Gillingham

NEMO

Nemo was playing with his fish friends, when suddenly he got caught in a net. He was trying to get out but he couldn't. He got put in a different part of the sea. He then saw his friend who helped him find his way home. Nemo was very happy.

KATY FORD (9)

Gillingham Primary School, Gillingham

BEAUTY THE BEAST

Beauty was lonely. She found a potion, she drank a bit. She started growing hair, and before she knew it, she was a beast! She found a dress. She thought it would hide her hair. She started crying. Beast walked in and gave her a potion to change back.

GRACIE DOWNER
Gillingham Primary School, Gillingham

UNTITLED

It was Christmas Eve. Shea and Kayla were
very excited. They went to bed early to wait
for Father Christmas. Suddenly they woke with
a start. Somebody was banging, it was Father
Christmas, he was stuck in the chimney! Kayla
and Shea helped pull him to safety!

KAYLA DUFFIELD

Gillingham Primary School, Gillingham

SLEEPING MOUNTAIN

The earth trembled, Ann-Marie careered to her window. A pot toppled, Ann-Marie dived for it. She caught it, put it back. She dashed back, looked out again. The sleeping mountain was certainly awake now. Lava and ash tumbled out, sending Ann-Marie and everyone near to death.

LOTTI PARFITT (11)
Gillingham Primary School, Gillingham

PUPPY TROUBLE!

I have two puppies. They're very mischievous. I
take them out for a walk every day.
One day I followed Rolo and found a hand, a real
hand in a trough! I rang 999, then stood there
open-mouthed. The police arrived. They were
nearly as shocked as I was ...

KAYLA BARRINGTON (10)

Gillingham Primary School, Gillingham

CINDERELLA'S FATHER GETS TRAPPED

Cinderella had been scrubbing dirty floors
since she was eight when her mother died.
Her stepsisters were lovely, they both tried to
convince her father to let her go to school and
have nice things, but he refused. So they decided
to trap him forever to die alone, unwanted.

JESSICA SWAFFIELD (10)

Gillingham Primary School, Gillingham

A HEALTHY SNACK

One day I went to a market stall. I bought an
apple. When I took a bite I had a heart attack.
Someone phoned an ambulance. They arrived in
minutes and took me to hospital. They looked
after me very well.
A month later I was discharged from the hospital.

JOSHUA GALE (9)

Gillingham Primary School, Gillingham

GHOST MANSION

In the old crooked mansion, red skeletons laid on the floor. The door creaked open, a shadow appeared, the floorboard creaked. Out came an old ghostly figure. We all were speechless, we couldn't move either! Out came another ghostly person. What would happen, would we survive?

JOSHUA NICHOLLS (10)

Gillingham Primary School, Gillingham

THE BEAR

I was standing there waiting for a grizzly bear to come gobble me up. I could hear the grizzly bear in the distance. He came stomping loudly, giving me a headache. I talked to him with a quiet whispering voice. In the end he was my friend and went home.

FRANCESCA HILL (9)
Gillingham Primary School, Gillingham

THE HAUNTED HOUSE

There was a house on a hill. Everyone said that it
was haunted. I didn't think it was.
But one night I went inside the house, I was
cold and wet. Out the corner of my eye, I saw
something. I screamed and ran all the way home!

SHANIA ANDERTON-GREEN (9)
Gillingham Primary School, Gillingham

HAUNTED HOUSE

I walked into the house. I crept up the creaky staircase. There was a mirror at the top of the stairs. Suddenly I saw another reflection in the mirror. The reflection wasn't my own. I didn't recognise the person. I quickly turned around. No one was there. I was frightened.

MOLLY WALKER (11)
Gillingham Primary School, Gillingham

DARK NIGHT

We walked into the room. A thin mist covered it. A blood-curdling scream echoed through the house. 'What was that?' he gasped.
'I don't know,' I said. A shape stirred in the corner of the room. It rose. Everyone screamed. It started to walk towards us. We ran away.

MATTHEW COOPER (10)
Gillingham Primary School, Gillingham

HUMPTY DUMPTY

There once was an egg called Humpty Dumpty.
He sat on a wall despite all the dangers, risks and
injuries that could happen. So he sat on the wall,
fell off and split in half. All the King's horses and all
the King's men could mend him. Lucky him!

JACK TOVEY (11)

Gillingham Primary School, Gillingham

HUMPTY DUMPTY

Humpty Dumpty was perched on a wall when all of a sudden he was on the floor. As soon as the King heard, he sent all his men and all his horses to put him together again. But it was just too difficult. Humpty Dumpty was broken forever and ever.

HANNAH RUSSELL (9)

Gillingham Primary School, Gillingham

GEORGE'S PERFECT MEDICINE

George was fed up. He decided to make a medicine. He collected his ingredients and a bowl. Next, George put all the ingredients into a bowl and stirred it up. George then gave it to his gran. She jumped up and grew, and was never mean again!

NATHAN WHITEHAND

Gillingham Primary School, Gillingham

THE EXPLODING SHIP

Chewie was fiddling with the ship's controls when he accidentally hit the lift-off button. The ship went whizzing up in the air. Chewie panicked! He saw bullets shooting behind him. Chewie dodged as many bullets as he could but then he got hit by one and the ship exploded.

EMILY WESTBY (9)
Gillingham Primary School, Gillingham

HUMPTY DUMPTY (RETOLD)

Humpty Dumpty was perched on a wall, Humpty
Dumpty suddenly fell. All the King's horses and
all the King's men had scrambled eggs for dinner
again! 'Bored, I want macaroni cheese!' said one.
I'll change it: Humpty Dumpty sat on a wall,
Humpty Dumpty didn't fall. OK? 'Yep, at last!'

EDEN MAIDMENT (9)

Gillingham Primary School, Gillingham

GEORGE'S MARVELLOUS MEDICINE

George was bored so he decided to make some marvellous medicine for his granny. He collected lots of ingredients and boiled them all together. He gave a spoonful to Granny. She began to grow taller and taller and taller and then smaller and smaller until she shrank and was gone!

PHOEBE NUNN (9)

Gillingham Primary School, Gillingham

THE COLT

I peered over the cliff face, craning my neck towards the sound. I heard it again. Then I saw it. I saw what it was. A ghostly vision of a pure white colt, trembling on a ledge on the cliff. I stumbled down to the trembling colt - but it vanished.

CHARLOTTE CRABB (9)
Gillingham Primary School, Gillingham

LITTLE RED RIDING HOOD

One day a little girl went to visit her granny who lived in the woods. She met a wolf who was hungry so he chased the little girl. She ran all the way to Granny's. Granny opened the door and slammed it in the wolf's face!

LEWIS PAYNE
Gillingham Primary School, Gillingham

CHICKEN LITTLE

Chicken thinks the sky is falling and rings the bell
in the town. He scares the rest of the town and
there is a load of trouble. Everyone rushes into
their cars and tries to get under cover. Chicken
is scared and hides under his bed. He's there all
night.

GEORGIA WATSON (10)

Gillingham Primary School, Gillingham

STELLA THE CHICKEN

Stella the fat chicken loves drinking and eating
burgers. She is lazy and clumsy. She spills ketchup
everywhere.
One day McDonald's was shut and she hated
KFC. She went back to her pen and ate all the
hay. She hated it so much she coughed and
spluttered then fell asleep.

GREGORY WHITE (9)

Gillingham Primary School, Gillingham

THE CURSE OF THE BARBARIAN BIGFOOT

'The Barbarian Bigfoot is a fib and lie.'
'Yeah right!'
'So why are we looking for it?'
'Because it's fun dude!'
'Watch out!' Then one of the men was thrown
down the cliff and hit the bottom. The Bigfoot
wrestled the other man. Who would win?

ADAM STARR (9)

Gillingham Primary School, Gillingham

THE GHOST

I went to school on a sunny day. It was a short walk. When I got there, I saw something floating. I went to touch it. It was cold. Everyone says it gets cold when a ghost is there. I said, 'Hello?' I trembled, waiting for a sound.

CASEY TOYE (9)

Gillingham Primary School, Gillingham

ME AND MY RAT ...

My rat is very cool but sadly he passed away a
week ago. I wish I had my rat back. We went
everywhere together. We went to the sunny
beach, the arcade, mean school, but the teacher
saw the rat, then fainted. I can't wait to
see him again.

LIAM STANDFIELD (10)

Gillingham Primary School, Gillingham

THE CURSE OF THE BLACK SERPENT

One peaceful day a young fisherman headed down to his father. 'Please can I come Father? I want to fish!'

'OK, but we'll be cautious!' yelled his father. When they were at Blackheart Lake the boy fell out of the boat. He heard a rattle. Was this now the end?

SEAN WALKDEN (9)

Gillingham Primary School, Gillingham

THE WATER GIANT

We sailed into the mists. Suddenly there was a noise. We stopped. Then a giant fist came out of the water, it was a water giant. It attacked ... was it the end of us?

ISAAC BEECHAM (8)

Gillingham Primary School, Gillingham

MY LIFE

I was standing there waiting for the three big elephants to come and stomp on me. I heard them in the distance. I couldn't believe it was me, there. They suddenly peered round the corner. The trees shook, the wind whimpered. I stood still and silent, still waiting there patiently.

OLIVIA FOWLES (9)

Gillingham Primary School, Gillingham

MERMAID SURPRISE!

Aysha looked out of her bedroom window. She lived right on the edge of a beach. She could see beautiful dolphins jumping in the blue glistening sea. Then she saw a tail rise up and she could see a mermaid! She thought that it was very, very mysterious.

JJ MACEY (9)

Gillingham Primary School, Gillingham

TWISTY NARNIAN TIME

At the station the kids felt magic. They found themselves on a volcano. They ran and tripped over a log. A vicious dwarf attacked them, but he took them to the King. He vowed to help them, but soon regretted it. He died and Peter became the great Narnia king!

LUKE MCELWAIN (9)

Gillingham Primary School, Gillingham

THE WIZARD AND HIS DOG

Once there was a young wizard. He had a dog called Zero.
One day they had a letter from the witch. She wanted a giant strawberry from the cliff. They climbed up the cliff and swiftly flew down. The witch was very happy and ate it in one big bite.

SASHA FITZGERALD (8)
Gillingham Primary School, Gillingham

ME AND MY PETS

I have lots of pets. I have a dog with twelve spots.
I have a cat with mauve stripes. I have fish with
scales, not whales. The mouse has run away, the
cat has followed.
I found the cat, she had swallowed the mouse,
but yeah she'd had kittens!

BETHANY BERRETT (8)
Gillingham Primary School, Gillingham

THE MONSTER UNDER MY BED

My mum said to me, 'There is no monster under your bed!'
As soon as the door closed I heard a shriek. I looked … *scratch!* I was gobbled up, pushed inside the monster's belly!

THOMAS ASHFIELD (8)

Gillingham Primary School, Gillingham

KAI AND THE DRAGON

I walked forward as the dragon roared fiercely.
I leapt back, I charged into the beast, but he
flapped his wings. The force of the air pressure
threw me to the other side of the dungeon. I hit
the wall and fell to the ground. I couldn't fight ...

KAI WHISTON (9)

Gillingham Primary School, Gillingham

GREEDY SANTA

One cold Christmas Eve, Santa slipped down
the gingerbread man's chimney as he slept by
the Christmas tree. Santa, getting hungry, picked
him up. Scared, the gingerbread man woke up,
jumped and ran out the door singing, 'Run, run,
as fast as you can, I am the Christmas gingerbread
man.'

SADIE LEWIS (9)
Holme St Cuthbert School, Mawbray

GOLDILOCKS AND THE THREE BEARS

One day three bears went for a walk. Goldilocks
went into their house, she ate all the porridge,
trashed the house and fell asleep in their beds.
Eventually the bears came home. They saw
Goldilocks and they had her for dinner for the
next three weeks.

JAANA BENNETT (11)
Holme St Cuthbert School, Mawbray

THE THREE LITTLE PIGS

There once were three little pigs and a big bad wolf. The three little pigs went to the farm but the big bad wolf followed them. Then when the three little pigs got to the farm, the big bad wolf had drunk all the milk!

AMY ARMSTRONG (10)
Holme St Cuthbert School, Mawbray

THE GINGERBREAD MAN II

The gingerbread man was getting married to
Sugar. They set off to the church on a sunny
morning. The church was beautiful with flowers
all around. It was spring so the lambs were
bouncing as they pulled the carriage. Once they
got married they had a party to celebrate.

AYESHA WISE (9)
Holme St Cuthbert School, Mawbray

THE HARE AND THE TORTOISE II

The hare and the tortoise had a race. The starter gun went *bang*, and off they went. The hare finished first. When the woodland creatures asked the hare why he had run so fast he said, 'I wasn't going to get caught making the same mistake as last time!'

EMMA LOFTUS (11)

Holme St Cuthbert School, Mawbray

JESSICA AND HER BEST FRIEND'S PICNIC

One sunny day Jessica sprung out of bed and made some sandwiches and cakes for her best friend, they were going on a picnic. Then her best friend arrived. 'Hello,' said Jessica. 'Hello, I have got everything we need.' They set off down the path, eating most of the food.

SAMANTHA CASSON (10)
Holme St Cuthbert School, Mawbray

LITTLE RED RIDING HOOD'S TALE

After Little Red Riding Hood left her grandma, she went off to see the world. She travelled with an owl and a pussycat in a pea-green boat. She went to a kingdom where it was constantly winter. She helped a lion defeat the witch and lived happily ever after.

HARVEY SMITH (7)

Holme St Cuthbert School, Mawbray

THREE BEARS

One day the three bears went out for a walk.
They left the door open. Goldilocks decided
to have a look in the bears' home. There was a
selection of porridge on the table. Baby's was the
best, then she went upstairs. There were three
beds. Baby's was the best.

REECE EDMONDSON (9)
Holme St Cuthbert School, Mawbray

UNBELIEVABLE!

The might of Liverpool are drawn against non-league Havant and Waterlooville in the FA Cup. An easy game for the reserves surely? Havant score first from a corner, then Liverpool equalise but Havant score again! Disaster, disaster! Can they hold onto their lead? What a match! Unbelievable!

OWEN JONES (9)

Penruddock Primary School, Penrith

OPERATION MARKET GARDEN

The artillery guns fire. Rats filled with germs hide in the bombed houses of the Dutch. Gliders glide, unheard over the enemy lines. The sound of a motor explodes, the scream of a dying man fades into the sound of gunfire. A house collapses ...
Now I'm trapped.

DOMINIC ROGERS (10)

Randlay Primary School, Telford

TITANIC

It was a clear, sunny day, it had been dreary earlier on. We were sailing through the Atlantic, then I saw it. We were heading for an iceberg. I screamed and ran back inside. The captain was drunk and said, 'Not to worry, we'll make a pitstop at that iceberg!'

DENZEL EFFIOM (11)
Randlay Primary School, Telford

NEVER FRIENDS

One hot day, a girl named Sayeh had a best friend
called Joanne. They both liked this boy called
Chris. In fact they both loved him, they never told
each other that they loved him. Then one day
they told each other and were never friends!

TAYYIBAH CHOUDHRY (10)

Randlay Primary School, Telford

PARENTS GONE

Dear Diary, it isn't long since my parents died and I'm still upset. I'm sorry I didn't write it in my diary till now because it was just so terrible. Anyway, all will be well since I'm going to live with my aunt, Cleo. I hope all will be well.

EUNICE WALKER (10)
Randlay Primary School, Telford

THE FRIGHTFUL NIGHT

Suddenly a ghost came out of nowhere. War started across two fields, fire and all sorts of elemental stuff. I was dead for sure, or would someone help me? The ghost guard went straight into me. The wizard saw me and everything went black. Goodbye world.

CHRISTOPHER BASKERVILLE (11)
Randlay Primary School, Telford

LOVE IS IN THE AIR

One scorching hot day, a teenage boy called Ollie and a sexy teenage girl called Cindy were sitting, perched on the green hillside, having a scrumptious picnic. As Ollie was munching his cheese in the radiant sunset, the girl leaned over him and kissed him. They lived happily ever after.

JAMES HEYWOOD (10)

Randlay Primary School, Telford

FLOOD

One day in London, many people were living their normal lives when the Thames Barrier opened and didn't close. That caused the Thames and the whole of London to flood. Many people died. Some escaped but were stuck in the tube for days.

THOMAS STEVENSON (10)

Randlay Primary School, Telford

STARRY, STARRY NIGHT

One night at midnight, heaps of stars burned to the ground with a crash and knocked all the houses down. Villagers called the builders to fix it but they said, 'Nobody can fix it ever again.' The villagers would have to be lonely on the atrocious, boring, old, busy street.

KAYLEIGH WAKEMAN (10)

Randlay Primary School, Telford

NIGHTMARE

Today was horrible, it's been seven days and I still
haven't been found! He won't let me go home.
I've been living on sausage rolls. He promised me
he would let me go. Seven days of hell! It's really
cold in this attic, freezing. Oh no, he's coming …

AMBER PHILLIPS (11)
Randlay Primary School, Telford

HOUSE OF TERROR

Lily came home from school. She saw a new
house with the words: *Terror House!* She went
in. She saw a mummy wrapped in bandages. Lily
screamed and disappeared!
'That will teach that girl for entering my house!'
The next day it was in the paper and on the news!

JADE VICCARS (9)
Randlay Primary School, Telford

77

ALIEN EXPERIMENT

One day Marcus got sucked up by an alien spaceship and they experimented on him. They turned him into an alien. They did another experiment on him.
The next day he was a baby alien. 'You're cute aren't you?' the alien said.

JOSHUA RIDGWELL (11)
Randlay Primary School, Telford

MONSTER MANIAC

I walked through my door and *bang!* Out jumped
a monster. So I ran out of my house and into the
shops. The man asked what was wrong so I told
him, afterwards I blacked out. But the back door
was open ... the monster ate me alive.

BRAD MITCHELL (9)
Randlay Primary School, Telford

THE HAUNTED HOUSE

One day I went upstairs and I saw a door that I had never seen before. I decided to open the door and inside there was a wicked witch. She looked surprised. She had a wand and she said, 'Abracadabra.' Then I heard a big fat noise.

DANIEL MORGAN (11)
Randlay Primary School, Telford

THE MONSTER

One day I met a monster. This monster was slimy and scary. I ran home up the creaky stairs. I locked the mouldy windows then I barricaded the doors with beds, lamps and lights. Then my mum shouted, 'Alex wake up, it's Christmas.' Oh it was just a dream.

ALEX BROWN (10)
Randlay Primary School, Telford

THE HAUNTED WOODS

Hannah and Michael were going for a picnic in the middle of the haunted wood. They found the perfect spot to set up the picnic. But before they could set anything up, a tree snatched Michael and Michael cried for help. But Hannah ran all the way home to Mummy.

JAY WHITE (9)
Randlay Primary School, Telford

RAINBOW DAY SURPRISE

Melissa was very excited, it was her birthday in two days! But she didn't dare ask for what she really wanted. She thought about it every day. It was in her mind all the time. Then one day she asked her mum. She got what she wanted, a rainbow slide.

CERI-ANN FIELD (10)

Randlay Primary School, Telford

MY DAY AT THE SAFARI PARK

One day my family and I visited the safari park. We saw the big elephants, zebras and white tigers. We went to see the creepy crawlies. My favourite bit was seeing the bats in the bat cave and the fantastic sea lion show. Smiling happily we went home for some tea.

AMELIA JONES (9)

Randlay Primary School, Telford

JANE THE ALIEN

Jane was an adventurous and spotty alien.
One day she went out for an adventure. She was
stuck on where to go. Whenever she couldn't
make up her mind she went to the kitchen and
asked her stressed mum. Mum said, 'Go and eat
the town.'
'OK,' said Jane.

NICOLA EDWARDS (8)
Randlay Primary School, Telford

CHRISTMAS EVE

One day Santa and his reindeer were delivering lots of presents. At one house they saw many decorations of him. Santa squeezed through the chimney and dropped off the presents. The children wrote to Santa to say the presents were great. Santa wrote back saying that he was very glad.

LOIS BARBER (9)

Randlay Primary School, Telford

SHREK THE HALLS

On Christmas Eve Shrek and his family were
eating slugs on toast, Donkey interrupted to drop
off presents. Shrek was surprised. Fiona said
'Calm down.' Fiona turned and said 'You can stay
if you're OK with the spare room.'
Donkey said 'OK,' and tried slugs on toast at the
table.

SAFFRON HALDRON (9)
Randlay Primary School, Telford

WHEN THE ALIENS CAME TO EARTH

Once upon a time I was playing football with my mates. Suddenly when I got the football, aliens came. I shot my football at them, it hit! They bounded back to their planet. My friend Adam picked me up and said, 'That was the best shot ever!'

ADAM HUSTWICK (8)

Randlay Primary School, Telford

JAMES BOND AND THE CRIME SCENE

One day there was a party going on but someone died! Who did it? Austin with his bat, Violet with her poisonous heart? Everybody screamed. James Bond ran outside to find the murderer, but who did the crime?

GABRIEL FILL (7)

Randlay Primary School, Telford

THE JOLLY GIANT

I'm a jolly giant, I own a flying saucer. Wait I'm
not meant to say this! How do you do? How do
you don't? How do you will? How do you won't?
How's your floors? How's your doors? How's
your roof?

CALLUM HANDY (7)
Randlay Primary School, Telford

LOVE AT FIRST GAZE

One shiny Monday this girl named Jayde had her
first crush, his name was Matthew. She jumped
out of bed, got changed, had breakfast and
skipped to school. When she got there she gazed
into his eyes then the bell rang.
Twenty years on it's still love at first sight.

HARLEY BINSLEY (7)
Randlay Primary School, Telford

THE FASTEST CAR IN THE WORLD

'Thanks for the tea love. Right let's get started,' said Dad excitedly. So I passed the spanner to him as I sipped my tea into my big belly. So we got to it, sparks went everywhere, tools flying and tears spilling, tyres popping. Finally we made the car.

ADAM REDDEN (10)

Randlay Primary School, Telford

A DREAM THAT BECAME A NIGHTMARE

One hot summer day I was walking along a beach and I decided to go for a paddle in the sea. It was really cold but then I was taken out to sea, it was horrible. I screamed … and then woke up.

LAURA WILKS (10)
Randlay Primary School, Telford

WIPEOUT

The burning sun hit his head as he dug for hours and hours. Finally his digging achieved his goal! He found a device, he pressed it, *kaboom!* The device wiped out the whole Earth.

ROY AU (10)
Randlay Primary School, Telford

UNTITLED

One dark gloomy night on Hallowe'en, a little boy went trick or treating. He gathered lots of sweets and was on his way home when he saw a church. He went up to it. The door was open. He crept through it. The door shut, the windows closed. He screamed!

PAUL FALLON
Randlay Primary School, Telford

LOST

One sunny day a girl called Grace was walking
through the woods. She was following a map.
Then the map flew out of her hands. She was
lost. Grace was wandering around for ages till she
found her map and followed it back home.

HANNAH MORGAN (10)

Randlay Primary School, Telford

MOONLIGHT TRAGEDY

One soundless, pitch-black night, the glittering moon had started to appear out of nowhere. It was as bright as a lightbulb with all the power in the world inside it. The moon's light was that powerfully intense, it managed to blind all the humans on this substantial universe.

JORDAN JONES (11)

Randlay Primary School, Telford

INVASION

Katie and Joe were playing with their toys. They were at the bit when the aliens were about to invade the world. So were the Zorg. They went to bed. In the night the toys came to life and invaded. They were attacking; would they survive? ... No one knew.

ZOE RICHARDS (10)
Randlay Primary School, Telford

WHERE AM I?

I suddenly wake up, not knowing where I am.
All I remember is me on a boat and a man with
a pistol. Suddenly an ear-splitting pain hits me
in the chest and I'm pushed off the boat. I can't
remember a thing and where am I?

LUCAS GRANT (11)
Randlay Primary School, Telford

THE TITANIC

It was a fine day. I had taken a stroll out onto
the deck. I screamed there was an iceberg dead
ahead. I sprinted up to the bridge and alerted the
captain. But it was too late. There was a sickening
crunch as we collided. A siren sounded. I ran.

DAVID STEPHENS (10)
Randlay Primary School, Telford

COCO'S VISIT TO SCHOOL

One day a slimy alien called Coco came to visit
Randlay Primary School. He made some new
friends. Coco ate all of his friend's lunches, even
the boxes. That wasn't enough, so he ate a huge
Christmas tree. He said goodbye and went home
to all of his old friends.

FFION JONES (9)
Randlay Primary School, Telford

HOLIDAY TO SPAIN

On holiday in Spain, my family and I went to
the beach. I swam out to sea with my brothers.
We saw millions of fish. There were quite a few
starfish and jellyfish. Then we swam back to shore
and my mum said, 'Go back to get something to
eat!'

JORDAN STUART (8)

Randlay Primary School, Telford

THE SUNNY DAY

One sunny day there was a boy and a girl who were on their way to an adventure park. When they got there the adventure park was a mess. It had been attacked by a two-headed dog. The dog came from his spaceship. He got them and ate them.

JESSICA SOMERVILLE (8)

Randlay Primary School, Telford

ROBOMAN AND CYBATRON

Three years ago, Man built the first thinking robot. The robot became a superhero. Suddenly he saw Cybatron in the distance. People screamed for help. Roboman kicked the robot. *Whack! Slam!* Roboman won the battle. The crowd cheered! Roboman flew away cheerfully and very happy.

FRED WALKER (8)
Randlay Primary School, Telford

NICOLA THE ALIEN

An alien called Nicola visited Earth. She knocked
on everybody's door to try to find a home to stay
in. At night she stayed in the dark, spooky park
where nobody went.
Next day Nicola found Hayley and she let Nicola
live in her home forever.

HAYLEY WESSON (8)

Randlay Primary School, Telford

PRESENTS FOR THE CHILDREN

One snowy Christmas Eve Santa visited Argos to get presents for the children. He looked in the catalogue and found brilliant toys for everyone. When he went to the shopkeeper behind the counter, the shopkeeper said, 'All of the presents have been sold out,' so everyone was upset.

KATIE BEDWORTH (8)

Randlay Primary School, Telford

THE TWO ROBOTS

There once was a robot called Rog. He was lonely. He worked for days and days but then it all changed. Another robot came down from Mars. Rog fell in love with the mysterious robot and got married. They lived happily on Mars and had a baby bot.

MATTHEW ROGERS (8)

Randlay Primary School, Telford

MIRACLE IN A NIGHT

Snowflake the polar bear said to some shivering penguins, 'I wish I could ride a magic sleigh.' Through the night a miracle happened. Snowflake woke up and the sleigh was in front of him. He jumped up in shock and jumped in the sleigh and rode magically around the world.

AIMEE KETTLE (8)

Randlay Primary School, Telford

SHREK'S POTION

One day Shrek was working on making a potion.
Shrek gave it to the dragon who turned into a pig.
Shrek made another potion, drank it and turned
into a baby. He went on the dragon and went
flying. They landed in a river.

FRANKIE MASON (8)
Randlay Primary School, Telford

THE MEAN MUM

Seeka Lannon's mum planned for her friend to steal her daughter and then pretend to find her so she could get the reward money. So she did it but couldn't find her! It turned out the man really was a kidnapper! So no money for her, or her daughter!

SHANNON KILLEY (11)

Rushen Primary School, Port St Mary

ALIEN SURPRISE

It was dark. I was walking home from trying to
find aliens and I'd had no luck, suddenly I heard
a bang. I hid in the bushes when a flashing light
blinded me. I couldn't see what was there. Finally
I could see again and thought I saw an alien ...

CHRIS POPE (11)
Rushen Primary School, Port St Mary

THE BIG MISTAKE

It was happening. The pump heaved and water spurted out. After 24 hours of pumping, it rose. Tall, elegant masts broke the surface, as the 300 year old ship rose. I was not looking at the ship, once used in battle. I was looking with terror at the coming stampede.

KATHRYN JENNINGS (10)
Rushen Primary School, Port St Mary

THE JAMMED ROLLER COASTER

Friday 13th of October I went to Blackpool for my birthday. I'd been on lots of roller coasters in my life, but this one was creepy - the loop was 210ft high. I was at the top and it jammed for 15 minutes over water! Luckily a helicopter came and rescued us.

ADAM TEESE (10)

Rushen Primary School, Port St Mary

113

DESERT ISLAND

I'm all alone on this island with the wind roaring in my face. Hours earlier I had been reading my favourite book, *Robinson Crusoe*. Suddenly I felt myself sucked into the book's heart and found myself on this desert island, and now I'm stuck here forever. How will I escape?

HAZEL MATTHEWS (11)

Rushen Primary School, Port St Mary

DISASTER STRIKES!

This year, my birthday treat was shopping in Wales. I had lots of money and was ready! We were on the way and suddenly it started raining really hard. My dad skidded and crashed into a house. That's all I remember of my thirteenth birthday. So much for shopping ...

ELLENA GILSON (10)
Rushen Primary School, Port St Mary

STRANDED

We'd left that horrible country and we were on the plane. We hit a bit of turbulence. I heard something hit the wing. I looked. It was an oil leak. I told the captain. He made an emergency landing in the desert. How would we get out of this desert?

JACK MAYLIN (10)
Rushen Primary School, Port St Mary

ESCAPE!

It's now 18th July 1943. We've been here for two months. A large group of German soldiers surrounded us and then threw us into a labour camp. There's been a shortage of food and water. A few of us are thinking of escaping. When it goes dark we plan our escape.

MAX HUGHES (10)
Rushen Primary School, Port St Mary

OUT COLD FOR LIFE

Friday 13th of April, a young girl was left alone in her house. Suddenly a burglar burst in through the window and threw an axe through the little girl's head.

Two days later the police were investigating. They found the little girl's ghost running around with an axe.

JAMES LAING (10)
Rushen Primary School, Port St Mary

DEAD HAND

On the haunted island Comaska, the fishermen were fighting. Their nets kept tangling together. David the bad guy chopped Doogie's hand off. He jumped in the water but there was no sign of it. Now they say it wanders on the beach ...

SHANNON FARAGHER (10)

Rushen Primary School, Port St Mary

ALL ALONE

It's nearly the end of the war, my family died by
the bombs. My house is destroyed. I have only
a little shelter. I can hear the bombs falling. Our
people are dying. I'm cold. I'm scared. I'm alone.

SARAH WIGNALL (11)
Rushen Primary School, Port St Mary

THE SNAKE

I was out riding my pony one night when suddenly a snake popped out from behind a tree. My pony spooked. I fell off and hit my head on a nearby tree. Faintly I saw my pony rearing in the horizon and gallop off. I lay there shivering.

MADDY ELLEY (10)
Rushen Primary School, Port St Mary

A DARK STARRY NIGHT

I was staring up at all the twinkling stars in the black night sky. All of a sudden, out of the blue, something came out of the sky. What was it? Was it a spaceship? Was it a plane or a star? Or maybe even a meteorite?

EVANGELINE HICKS (10)
Rushen Primary School, Port St Mary

GHOSTLY THINGS

In a dark creepy tower, there were two boys
called Adrian and John. Adrian and John went into
the tower and they saw something moving on the
wall. 'What was that?' said Adrian.
'I think it was that mirror over there.'
'Aaah! It's a ghost!'
'A ghost?' said John ...

MICHAEL COOK (10)

Rushen Primary School, Port St Mary

NOT ALONE

As I got home I heard a sudden move from behind me. I quickly turned the key, got in and locked the door. Then it happened again, but on the roof. It wouldn't stop. There was a bang on the roof. My heartbeat got faster ...

KYLE SUSAYA (11)
Rushen Primary School, Port St Mary

A SPACE ADVENTURE

There were two boys called Tom and Bob. They loved space and they won a competition to go into space. So they went to the space centre. Then in the spaceship. '3, 2, 1, blast-off!' But they disappeared ... to be continued.

NATHAN PATRICK (10)
Rushen Primary School, Port St Mary

A NORMAL DAY AT CHURCH

I was on my way to church, talking about the new stained glass window. We all settled down on the pews. The vicar started telling us the hymns. *When* … a monster broke through the new window. 'Ahhh!' we all shouted, not in unison. But the monster shouted back …

MICHELLE JAMIESON (11)
Rushen Primary School, Port St Mary

THE CHRISTMAS CURSE

It all started a long time ago, but it still hurts me.
It was Christmas Day. Everything was going great
until the cracker was pulled. A big explosion
erupted and the house was falling. Everyone was
frantic. A brick fell killing Dad. It was then that I
knew I was cursed.

DANIELLE AKITT (11)
Rushen Primary School, Port St Mary

LUCINDA'S MUM

Once there was a girl called Lucinda who had a
witchy Mum. One day when she got home the
house had burnt down. She heard a scream and
found her mum on the grass screaming. Was she
OK? Lucinda ran over to her mum. She had no
pulse.

ISABEL O'ROURKE (11)
St Francis Catholic Primary School, Nailsea

THE MIRACLE OF THE CENTURY

Suddenly with a *phut* the engines stopped. Even though I could see the airport I knew I would be lucky to survive. We raced towards the ground, slow at first, but then like a rocket in space. We were going fast! As my heart stopped it happened ...

CHRISTOPHER ROBERTS (11)
St Francis Catholic Primary School, Nailsea

SPEED OF LIGHT

Last lap, sweat pouring down my head. Second
and can't get out. The long bend is coming, the
radio transmitter blasting.
'Use the Nitrous, it's the only way!' but I couldn't.
I'd hit leading car and be knocked out the race.
Some say it's impossible. But it had to be …

KIERAN MATLEY (10)

St Francis Catholic Primary School, Nailsea

STRANDED

Help we are stranded on this magical island.
I might soon die because there is nothing to
eat. We are communicating with you with old
technology. Please come and get us. Ahh help me,
SOS the monster has returned. *Beep, beep!*
'Barry we need to kill that beast,' said Johny.

AMBROSE ROBERTS (10)
St Francis Catholic Primary School, Nailsea

MY ADVENTURE

Once I found a teletransportation device at school. I was transported to King Ansuke's castle. He wanted to destroy a ghost. After a long fight we managed to suck him up into a vacuum cleaner. I missed my lessons but I returned in time for my mum to collect me.

ROBERT GUTIERREZ (10)
St Francis Catholic Primary School, Nailsea

LOST IN THE JUNGLE

Lost in the jungle, great! I frantically swung my machete at hanging leaves and reeds. The sun beat down on me. *Sss, Sss, Sss.* What was that noise?

Only two people ever returned from the Jungle of Doom. The further you go in, the more evil, deadly demons you'll encounter.

JAMES ALEXANDER (10)
St Francis Catholic Primary School, Nailsea

HORROR TIME AWAITS

There are moments when my mind misses beats.
I'm out in the street on my own. Footsteps heard
as I walk along. I swear someone is following me
but who? I arrive at the grave, scared to death!
Argh! Sucks my blood, leaves me there dying and
leaves alone.

SEHAR RAZA (10)

St Francis Catholic Primary School, Nailsea

GINGERBREAD GIRL AND THE ATTACK OF THE COOKIE MONSTER

Gingerbread Girl lived at the bottom of Candy Mountain with her dog Gumdrop. But one day the cookie monster that lived at the top of Candy Mountain stole Gumdrop. So she went to rescue Gumdrop. She climbed to the top of Candy Mountain and was captured by the cookie monster.

ISOBEL BRITTON (11)
St Francis Catholic Primary School, Nailsea

HE WHO MUST NOT BE NAMED

He told me not to open it, but it was my only choice. Suddenly, something came shooting out. It was him, he spoke, 'I will seek revenge!'
Then I knew I was trapped forever with no way out, but I had to do it. I had to …

EMMA WOOD (10)
St Francis Catholic Primary School, Nailsea

CAUCASIAN HERDING DOG

I'm a Russian herding dog, I protect my owner's sheep. It is dark, the night is very still, suddenly I hear the noise. The wolves are coming. I see the leader heading for my sheep. I attack and kill him. That is why I am known as the wolf killer.

BILLY DAVIS (10)
St Francis Catholic Primary School, Nailsea

A VISIT TO THE KENNEL

There once was a dog that had a special power
- invisibility. He could disappear, even on his
owner's walk. His owner, sadly had gone to Spain
so the dog had to go to the kennel. He was in his
kennel and not enjoying it when, *ping!* Where had
he gone?

TJ JAMES (10)
St Francis Catholic Primary School, Nailsea

BENEATH THE SURFACE

Now the waves were consuming the *Skimwater* as
it trudged along. But with Alex at the wheel they
didn't stand a chance! Already things were going
badly when suddenly they got worse.
Thump! Thump! Thump!
Alex swirled around to find a dark shadow
looming towards him. His heart raced. 'No!'

RICCARDO ENOCH (11)
St Francis Catholic Primary School, Nailsea

SANTA'S SURPRISE

Santa arrived at the final house to find there were
no more presents. He wondered how he could
have forgotten three presents. Then he read the
letter that the children had written …
It said, 'Dear Santa, we don't want any presents
but can we have a sleigh ride please? Thanks.'

KIRSTY STEAD (10)

St Francis Catholic Primary School, Nailsea

AROUND THE PAVING STONE IN 80 HOURS

There once was a snail called Sweeney who thought he could walk across a paving stone in 80 hours. So he went on his journey and he saw a leaf, then another, then another. He also made a friend called Lenny! He also completed his challenge! Hoorah!

REBECCA HAYLES (10)

St Francis Catholic Primary School, Nailsea

THE SECRET MAZE

Jack dashed to the left. He dashed to the right.
'No one will ever find me here,' whimpered Jack,
then it hit.
It was big, hairy with fangs. It had red eyes. Jack
skidded forward. Dead end. He couldn't do it.
Then it pounced. Jack jumped up ...

CHRISTOPHER GREEN

St Francis Catholic Primary School, Nailsea

CORE

Doctor Joe strolled in the lab. In his hand was a test tube full of green liquid. The doctor dropped a magical bath bomb in, which fizzed and bubbled. A rumbling sound echoed around the world. 'That wasn't supposed to happen!' he screamed. The world opened at its core!

LAUREN TYE (10)
Shifnal Primary School, Shifnal

BIGFOOT!

We were in our cabin in North America. It was cold and snowing. I saw a brown blur in the distance between the trees. The figure was getting bigger and closer. I was more curious than scared. What was it? It smiled and waved. Bigfoot! No longer a legend.

CHELSEA WATSON (9)

Shifnal Primary School, Shifnal

STAR WARS CARTOON

One day Anakin went for a ride on his rider. He got to the cave, he saw Dooku. He was planning for world domination. Meanwhile C3PO and R2-D2 got a hand from Obi-Wan, almost stopped Dooku and his apprentice Grievous from taking over the great superior Jedi race.

NATHAN WILLIAMSON (10)
South Trelawny Primary School, Devon

THE STRANGE FIGURE

It was a cold, foggy winter's evening. In the fog
I saw a strange figure. I screamed and started
to run. The figure ran after me. I could hear the
feet running behind me, the sound of its breath
panting. Then it ran past me. Oh it was my dog!

THOMAS OWEN (10)
South Trelawny Primary School, Devon

THE GIRL IN THE DARK

Roaming through the deserted house, Elizabeth, step by step, moved ever closer to the room ahead. Suddenly, Elizabeth turned around. The door had slammed shut. The darkness had certainly got on her nerves so, she barged the door and finally reached her destination. The dinner table for food and drink.

BEN SHIELS (10)
South Trelawny Primary School, Devon

THE NIGHTMARE BEFORE CHRISTMAS

On Christmas Day I came home and I went into the lounge to watch TV. Before I turned the TV on, I heard a loud bang from next door. I went to see what the big bang was. A ghost watching TV! It was going to eat me! I ran ...

KIERAN OAKLEY (8)

Springfield School, St Saviour

THE LOST CAVE

One night I was lost in a dark, gloomy cave. I was so scared then I heard, *drip, drip.* Suddenly a pink fluffy monster jumped out. I shouted, 'aargh!' I quickly ran, but it was my dad dressed up ...

WILLIAM EMERSON (8)
Springfield School, St Saviour

THE OLD WOODEN HOUSE

Rose opened her door. There was silence and Rose heard a creak on the stairs. She saw red eyes poking out of the painting on the wall and she screamed to death. Then she saw an old lady doing some sewing by the fire and said, 'How are you lady … ?'

DEANNA DE LEMAS COOPER (9)

Springfield School, St Saviour

ONE STORMY NIGHT

It was a cold and rainy day and Bethany was stuck outside. She was scared and lonely. 'I want to go home!' Bethany shouted. Then out of a tree came an old lady that took her to a little house out of nowhere and brought her up …

BETHANY MOISAN (8)
Springfield School, St Saviour

WHAT WAS THAT?

Kate was walking to school, then she heard a rustling in the leaves. 'What was that?' Kate said. She looked over her shoulder to see what it was, but there was nothing there. She carried on walking, feeling confused.
The next day the same thing happened. Then she saw it!

ELISHA HART (9)
Springfield School, St Saviour

WHERE IS MY DOG?

One night a dog got lost, he was terrified.
In the morning the little boy cried his eyes out.
Then Mum and Dad rushed into the room and
said, 'What happened?'
'The dog was sleeping on my bed and now he is
gone.'
'Don't worry, he will return.'

RYAN ECCLES (8)
Springfield School, St Saviour

THE UNEXPECTED ARRIVAL

Suddenly it all went dark and quiet and then I felt the plane scarily sinking from the sky. I heard a thunderous thud.
I looked out of the window and to my surprise, I was in sunny, beautiful, hot Hawaii. Wow! We had not crashed at all.

SAM HUDDLESTON (9)

Thwaites School, Millom

THE HAPPENING

I thought it was going to be a normal day. But I was wrong. As I was walking towards the food court. I rounded the corner of my chalet and there it was, coming closer and closer. The warthog came closer still, then it licked me and ran away.

ISAAC STREET (10)

Thwaites School, Millom

THE TREASURE!

I was blinded by the sun, a giant emerald! I couldn't dig anymore but I had to, so I seized my shovel and began again. Was there anything to be found? After a while I hit something, it was hard … was it the treasure I had been searching for?

SIMRAN RANAMAGAV (10)
Wolvey CE Primary School, Wolvey

THE TREASURE

Me and my friends were playing pirates, until something fell on me. It was a treasure map! Near a tree was an 'X'. We dug every single tree in my back garden. After lots of digging my shovel banged into something. Could it be the treasure?

RENEE LAWATI (10)
Wolvey CE Primary School, Wolvey

THE DEVIOUS PIRATE

One scorching hot day a devious pirate was frantically digging for gold, under the treacherous sea. It was guarded by a vicious shark. He had a little knife in his pocket. He killed the shark. He got the treasure. There was a gold cup and a gold necklace!

RYAN JONES (10)

Wolvey CE Primary School, Wolvey

DIGGING FOR TREASURE

The heat was unbearable, the captain was pacing
up and down impatiently and excited. Suddenly
my shovel clanked against something hard, I knelt
down on my knees and started to claw the earth
around the object. The captain was observing me
like a hawk. Was it the treasure?

RACHEL FAULKNER (10)
Wolvey CE Primary School, Wolvey

UNTITLED

Harshly tied around my eyes was a blindfold. The last thing I saw was the shark-infested sea. The starving sharks were waiting for their next meal.
Me!

LUKE FOSTER (10)
Wolvey CE Primary School, Wolvey

THE QUEST FOR TREASURE

'Ouch!' the sun was burning me while I was looking for treasure. There was the sight of sensational gold. However, as I glanced over the gentle sand, there it was, the treasure that I had been searching for. I darted over in lightning speed. I started crawling down, under sand.

JOSHUA BROWN (11)

Wolvey CE Primary School, Wolvey

FRANTIC CAPTURE

I began digging frantically in the scorching sun, for treasure! Before the other mighty pirates arrived. However, it was too late, they were here! (What was I going to do?) Trying to sprint away through the thick sand, one of the ghastly pirates captured me! I was trapped …

BETHANY BROWN (11)

Wolvey CE Primary School, Wolvey

THE PLANK

I envisaged myself going off the end of it, for what
I'd complained about, how stupid was I to betray
my shipmates?
'Get to it, he's walking the plank tonight.'
This was the moment I'd been dreading. *Splash!* In
I went.
'Ha-ha. Another one dead.'

LOUISE ELLIOT (10)
Wolvey CE Primary School, Wolvey

SPANISH CLASS

I was late for Spanish class. The teacher was cross and told me off. She asked how we say ice cream in Spanish. I started daydreaming about a chocolate ice cream sundae, with chocolate sprinkles! Delicious! The teacher asked me for the answer. 'Helados!' I replied, with a huge smile.

ELEANOR REDDEN (9)

Wootton Primary School, Wootton

MORNING

The girl woke suddenly. A dark, strange figure was standing over her. She gasped in horror and was frozen with terror. She tried to scream but no sound came out of her mouth. She quickly flicked on her lamp and her sister exclaimed, 'It's morning! Time to get up!'

ELIZABETH REDDEN (11)

Wootton Primary School, Wootton

TRAPPED

Trapped where? You may ask. I'll tell you, I'm stuck in a tall, gloomy and dark tower with dusty, stringy cobwebs hanging from the ceiling and hairy spiders crawling up my back. All there is, is me, the spiders and the empty barren landscape. Footsteps! Who do they belong to?

NAOMI PLATT (10)
Wootton Primary School, Wootton

BELLA!

Callum and Cassey loved their dog Bella! But one day she went missing. They were really upset and wanted their much-loved dog back. They searched high and low. Suddenly Cassey gasped, then giggled, Bella was snuggled up in the cloakroom. With loads of newborn puppies!

LYDIA MIDDLETON (11)

Wootton Primary School, Wootton

SURPRISE BIRTHDAY

It was Joe's birthday, wow! What a great surprise birthday party, he saw his old friends. What a great day! He got lots of gifts. 'Amazing!' he shouted as he opened them. 'What a lovely day! Thanks everybody,' said Joe. All of his friends enjoyed themselves, had lots of fun.

AMANTLE OTUKILE (10)
Wootton Primary School, Wootton

THE QUEEN ELEANOR

One evening, me and Georgina went to the pub for a meal. We went to wash our hands, when suddenly the mirror sucked us up and carried us to Queen Eleanor's home. She wanted to cut our heads off but just as the blade came down, we zoomed right back.

EMILIE GIBBS (10)

Wootton Primary School, Wootton

169

MAROONED!

I was on a cruise, when suddenly we hit
something. I looked over the side of the boat and
I saw a rock scraping along the edge of the boat.
Water was pouring in, I was stranded on an island.
But I was eventually rescued and got home safely.

JAMIE OSBORNE (10)
Wootton Primary School, Wootton

VICTORY

Injury time in the big cup game, Norwich must score. The roaring crowd shout for victory. It's pouring with rain, the Palace goalkeeper slips on the slippery, sloping pitch. Lita curves the ball in the net. The whistle goes and Norwich win the cup.

ASHLEY SCOTT (8)

Wootton Primary School, Wootton

DINOSAUR

Jane ran outside. Suddenly she saw a figure.
Bravely she ran for it. 'Hello Jane and now
refrain,' a witchy voice chanted! Jane was in a
desert. A dinosaur chased her! *Help*, thought
poor Jane. More dinosaurs chased her …
She woke up in her bed the next morning. What
an adventure!

HANNAH SIMMONITE (9)

Wootton Primary School, Wootton

HAUNTED HOUSE

Jimmy was running through the haunted house. He heard a weird sound. It came from up the spooky staircase. He had a look in a small room. Suddenly he heard the noise behind him, Jimmy turned quickly, to find his brother playing a trick! Then they went home for spaghetti.

DANIEL SHORE (9)
Wootton Primary School, Wootton

SPIDER

It was a very sunny day, I was picking flowers on a meadow. There were lots of beautiful flowers. 'Ohhh!' There was a black, horrible spider. I was terrified, I ran to tell Mum. She said 'You just imagined it.' But I know that I saw that massive creature.

JULIA STACHOWSKA (11)
Wootton Primary School, Wootton

BEING GOOD OR NAUGHTY

There was a little boy who could be very naughty.
But one day he didn't want to be naughty, so he
tried to make all the right choices to be good and
everyone was very pleased. He realised that being
good gave him all nice feelings and he liked that.

CONOR CARR (9)

Wootton Primary School, Wootton

INFORMATION

We hope you have enjoyed reading this book - and that you will continue to enjoy it in the coming years.

If you like reading and writing, drop us a line or give us a call and we'll send you a free information pack. Alternatively visit our website at www.youngwriters.co.uk

Write to:
Young Writers Information,
Remus House,
Coltsfoot Drive,
Peterborough,
PE2 9JX

Tel: (01733) 890066
Email: youngwriters@forwardpress.co.uk